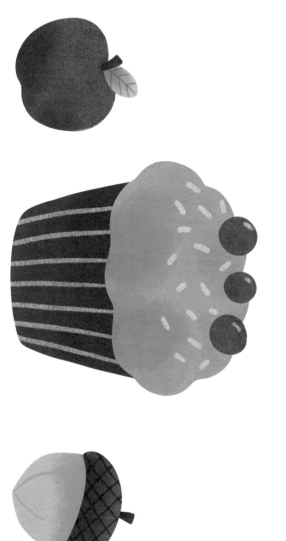

I LOVE FALL

Find our books at Amazon, Barnes & Noble, Walmart, Books-A-Million, OverDrive, Kobo, Lulu, IngramSpark, and more!

Like, Share and Follow us on Facebook, Instagram, Threads, Pinterest, YouTube, LinkedIn, and more! Find our Sloths Love to Read Podcast on Spotify, Apple Podcast, Amazon Music, Pandora, and more!

www.SlothDreamsBooks.com

Text Copyright © 2023 by KeriAnne N.Jelinek
Illustrations Copyright © 2023 to KeriAnne N.Jelinek & Sloth Dreams Books & Publishing, LLC.

Published by Sloth Dreams Books & Publishing, LLC.
Sloth Dreams Children's Books
Pennsylvania, USA
www.SlothDreamsBooks.com

All Rights Reserved.
ISBN: 978-1-7417-8330-8

I Love FALL

By Coral & KeriAnne Jelinek

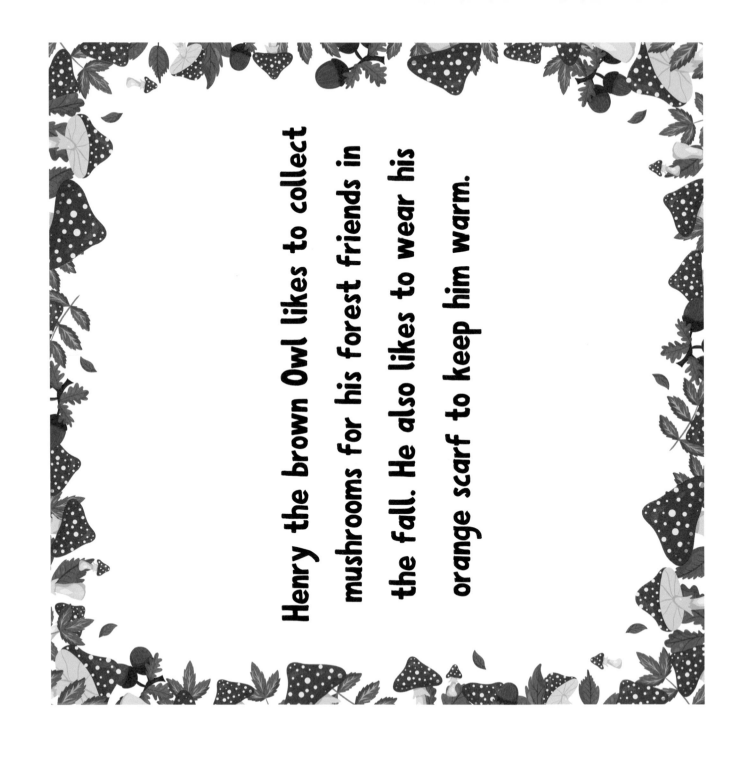

Henry the brown Owl likes to collect mushrooms for his forest friends in the fall. He also likes to wear his orange scarf to keep him warm.

Cornelius the brown bear loves to sip his hot chocolate during the cold fall mornings. He wears his warm orange scarf and snuggles in his red and white spotted blanket to keep warm.

Piper the little brown mouse likes to collect delicious apples during the fall. She loves her beautiful blue scarf.

Ruby the ladybug loves to go for walks during the crisp fall afternoons. She is excited when she explores pretty colored leaves.

Flora the red fox loves to sit on old tree stumps in the sun. She feels extra special wearing her red and white checkered bandana around her neck.

Luna the gray raccoon loves to bake blueberry pies during the fall. She loves her purple sweater because it matches the color of the blueberries in her pies.

Henrietta the hedgehog loves to take long naps on her big pile of fall leaves. She wears her red polka-dot scarf to keep warm in the cold fall afternoons.

Maya the little brown squirrel loves to nibble on plump red mushrooms during the fall. She likes to wear her pink sweater to keep warm on cold fall evenings.

Bixby the tan bunny loves to discover new foods. She loves to eat pumpkins in the fall. She also enjoys wearing her pink polka-dot scarf at dusk.

Mabel and Fred enjoy climbing to the top of the tallest mushrooms to sleep during the fall nights. They love their blue and pink fancy bowties.

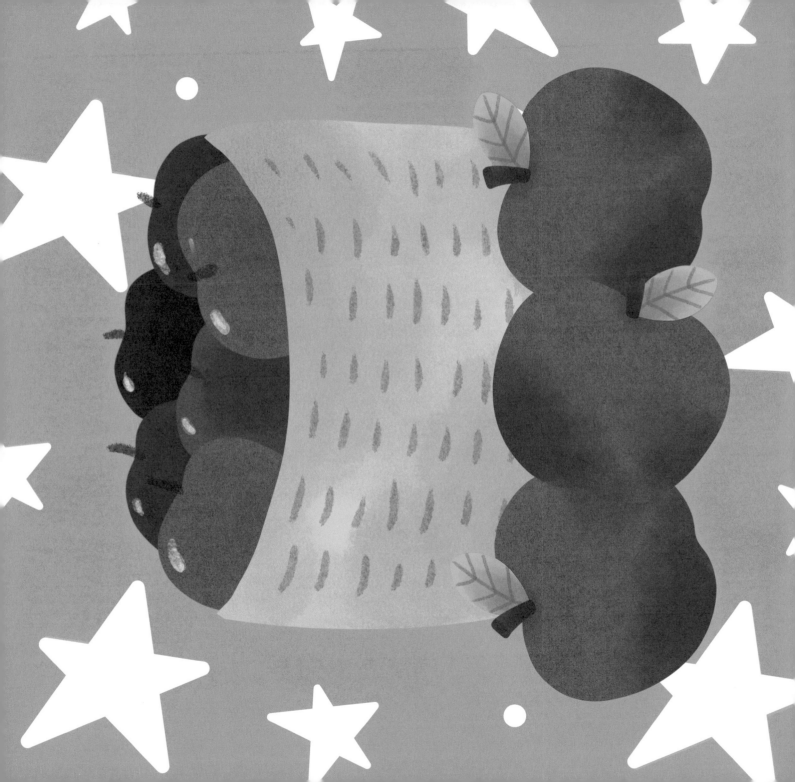

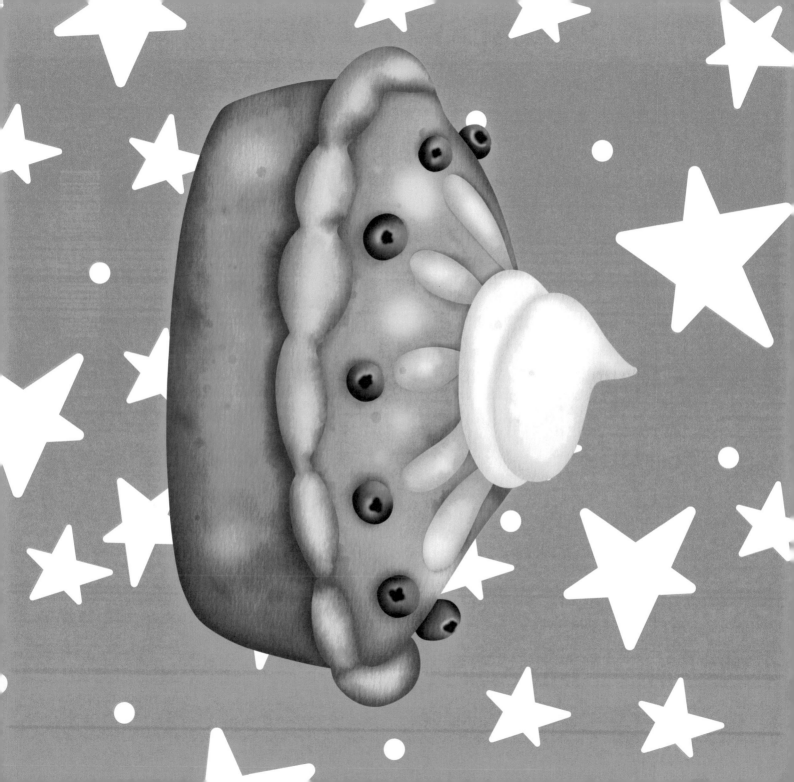

23287629R10017